cash 4 gold

I0777103

SEASON OF THE RAT

ELIZABETH HALL

Cash 4 Gold Books

www.c4gbooks.com

ISBN: 979-8-9907275-3-3

Cover & interior design: Tex Gresham

I don't know when I first noticed the rat living in my apartment. Maybe it was summer. Back then I was easily confused. The sound of claws on the roof was or was not the scraping of a sagging palm frond. In my bed, I strained to hear what sounded like scurrying above my head. I called out to my roommate, Did you hear that? *Mark said,* Not really, *then,* Maybe. *He said,* Call the landlord if you want. *Mark knew me long enough to know I wouldn't call the landlord. Not without more evidence. I waited. I smoked out the window. I both dreaded and anticipated the rat's return. I told friends, I'm creeping myself out every night, and I like it. Yet, whenever I heard a scratch, I shot up in bed, breath caught. I wanted to confirm that what I heard the first night was true: a rat was living on my roof. Alone. It rarely slept. In this, we shared something in common. During the night I never heard it rest.*

1. RAT BEACH

Fall 2018

When I can't sleep, I walk to the beach. Black breakwater banked by sand. If I dig my foot in deep, I find plain dirt beneath. I sit under a palm. That's all I do: sit and watch the water slosh.

In the Southern California landscape, the huge white waves of the surf cities get all the glory. Here, in San Pedro, at the port of LA, there are no waves. Most nights there is no one on the beach but me. Out past the tide pools, in the crevices of the bluffs, people are housing themselves, eating, dreaming, texting, and tending their cats. Sometimes a small truck with city decals drives over, shines two headlights on the water and drives off. Other times the driver rolls down the window and asks me questions. These encounters are rare. More often I encounter rats. I startle them. If I see one at all, I see it fleeing.

The roof rat is different. Night after night I study its presence. I consult a checklist on an exterminator website, "Signs You Have a Problem." Scratching noises? Yes. "Squeaking?" Yes. "Running sounds?" Uh huh. In my mind, rats dwell in sewers and subway tunnels, sometimes at the beach, but never high on tiled roofs, in the trees, so near the moon.

What little I know about rats is informed by books and cartoons. In these narratives, rats rarely play a starring role, much less the hero. More often they're cast as greedy sidekicks, trash-eating precursors of doom. Think of the rapacious, yellow-toothed rodents in George Orwell's *1984*. But as I lie in bed listening, I struggle to believe the animal living in my roof resembles those monstrous literary creatures. For one, my rat appears to live alone, not in a tangled nest of knotted tails; I hear four feet running, never more than four Which defies what I once understood to be basic rat logic: rats live in packs. *Do some rodents live alone?* I type into my phone and wait for the night to light up with facts.

It is true that I am easily confused.

Some weeks ago, before discovering the rat, I drove to the desert, a place I visit as often as possible. On this trip, I pitched a tent against two sandstone boulders. My roommate, Mark, and our friend, Sean, built a fire and cooked red beans in a black pot. Wind made the flames vibrate blue and white. Owls hooted. We looked at the night sky, sure we were seeing every single star. I swallowed two blue pills,then lay down alone in my tent. I wanted the stars to pulse. If only for a night. I watched them through the mesh slit at the top of the tent. It was those pulsing stars, those traces of bright white light, I focused on when I was awakened in the middle of the night. At first I thought a rodent was rooting around outside my tent. Then I heard the *shhhh* of the door's zipper slowly coming undone. The nylon floor crackled. I lay still. I played dead like an animal. When I woke in the morning, there were no physical traces of what had happened the night before on my body or outside the tent. Though I looked.

On the drive back from the desert, I rode shotgun, head against the window. Mark gripped the wheel with both hands. Cautious as ever, he toed the speed limit all the way back to L.A. I knew we were home when I saw the billboard with the lawyer and his German Shepard. Soon I would be alone in my room, or so I thought. A few days later the rat appeared.

Unlike the beach rats, or the rats I sometimes see in the street, I cannot ignore the roof rat. My rat. It has entered my scene. It has crowded the frame. Once aware of the rat's presence, I'm never not aware of it.

A space of imagined nothingness, the desert offers many routes to find and lose oneself. Some of the paths I've pursued: drop acid in a flat of chollas. Hike. Stare at the sky for hours on end, past the stars, into the cosmos.

Climb a mountain. Throw up red wine. Write poems in the sand. Die one warm night in a tent, owls hooting.

In Alejandra Pizarnik's poem *Fear*, the narrator discovers she is dead yet still feels fear:

> fear in a black hat
> fear hiding rats in my blood

I'm so struck by the cold precision of Pizarnik's lines, those rats running in her blood, I stay awake all night reading, arrive late to work at the library. I don't find any more poems about rats, but I find one about me: "When you're dead, you're dead, for all the smiling you do."

I smile, eyes puffed purple in the fluorescent library lights. Early morning shift. *Hiiii!* I say to every kid who walks through the library's double doors for story time. In between sips of instant coffee, I shelve books. The coffee passes through my throat and intestines, touching none of my nerves. If anyone asks about my eyes, I blame the rat. *It runs all night*, I say. In bed, stiff as a matchstick, I watch the hours burn.

If I ever want to sleep again, I know I need a plan. The problem isn't the rat itself, but how I think about the rat. I pursue change the only way I know how: I open one book then another.

No one's encouraging me to report the rat. Especially not Mark, or Sean, who spends most evenings at our apartment. When I complain about the noise, Mark narrows his red eyes and exhales a big puff of smoke. He says, *You are the master of your own destiny*. He laughs, and I laugh, too, as if on cue. We both understand the value of saying as little as possible to the building manager.

It's true I don't hear the rat if I let the box fan blow at full blast. If I focus on the yellowed page. In my lap, an article about rat socialization that I printed at the end of my library shift. *We've gotten rats wrong all these years*, the authors tell me. Survival isn't the only, or even primary, reason rats cohabitate and fraternize. They do not socialize randomly but show strong, trackable preferences to spend time with specific rats while avoiding others. Their preferences do not appear to be related to mating or the rat's rank within the rat world hierarchy. The impulse to survive alone can't explain their connections. I flip to the last page. I want more. But there's no more to read tonight.

The vibrations wake me. It's too early in the morning to listen to Mark plug and unplug amps with Sean in the living room. I throw on my jacket and climb the hill behind my building. The flowers in my neighbor's yard look fake. I pluck one off its stalk to check. I lean over the fence and pull a pomelo from a leathery branch. Inside the rind is thick and white. I shred it with my thumbnail and wait for the day to begin.

Soon after my trip to the desert, I find myself looking for new friends. I meet Rachel at a ramen shop after my shift at the library. We sit along a red wall, which casts a pink glow across our faces. She tells me she's in LA to finish her dissertation on architectural conservation in Israel. *In some places, they used a historically accurate brick that is now rapidly disintegrating due to climate change*, she says. *The bricks are self-destructing.* She rolls up her sleeves and blows the steam off her bowl. Once the salty broth hits me, I have trouble paying attention to anything else. After a loud slurp, I stop. Hoping to impress her, I talk about the ruins from a socialist colony in the desert outside Palmdale. *We should go*, she says. In the parking lot, she asks, *When.* I say, *Any time I can catch a ride.*

My apartment, like all the others Mark and I've rented in the city, is small enough to hear each other through the walls. Night after night I listen to him unlock the front door, take off his shoes, rip the plastic off a frozen pizza, open the oven. I feel the heat slowly rise through the crack at the bottom of my bedroom door. I smell the sweet diesel of fresh weed. His smoke fills the hall, mixing with my own. I breathe it in. No other way.

A good apartment is hard to find. This is one thing I learned after I ended my ten year relationship with Mark last year. The morning after our break up, I laid in bed scrolling through apartment ads on my phone while Mark slept next to me. By the time he woke, I was no longer searching for studios on the city's edge. I was typing, "Is it toxic to live with an ex?"

Later that evening we sat down at the kitchen table and decided to platonically cohabitate. We mouthed the words "open communication" and "clear boundaries." We wrote the house agreements on a yellow pad.

One bedroom apartments in L.A. rent for an average of $2,545/month. On Curbed, I read that Angelenos must earn $74,371/year to live comfortably in the city while the average annual pay for a full-time employee is $46,425. My face burns as I read. Unsurprisingly, two-thirds of L.A. renters struggle to afford their housing. This phenomenon extends beyond California. Harvard researchers found that nearly half of the U.S.'s 44.0 million tenants are cost-burdened, meaning they spend 30% or more of their income on rent. My anger rises with each paragraph. Anger and newfound intimacy. I realize that 22 million strangers and I have something in common.

The apartment I share with Mark is a shotgun. To reach my room, I must walk through his room, and to get to the bathroom, he must walk through my room. The hall is lined with broadsides that say, "EAT ASS BE FREE." An unposted house rule says no overnight guests, romantic or otherwise, without discussion. There are signs the rules are shifting. One week I find a red barrette I don't recognize sitting on the bathroom counter. In the mornings I sometimes hear the front door open and close right as my alarm plays the opening riff of *Bad to the Bone*. These nearly imperceptible shifts. I wait for the evidence to pile up.

2. ROMANCE AND THE RAT

Dazzle of a new day, a hollowed rind filled with dew. A license plate on the freeway that says RATLORD. Late March and I borrow Mark's car to drive to Irvine for the afternoon. I've booked an appointment at the university archives where I plan to shiver at a long wooden table and thumb through the personal papers of Robert F. Gentry, the first openly gay elected official in Southern California. But I miss the turn off the freeway. I drive towards the coast, telling myself it's far too nice a day to read inside.

At the park, the wind drowns out the cars. Beyond the tree break, I sit in the dry grass and spit cherry pits. I let my skirt fill with twigs. A child grabs a blue ball and drops it. A cloud of dirt rises. The child tries to throw the ball. It falls. I turn a page, and the breeze blows it back. I read the same lines about rats' motley appetites. Here, a rat stands against a stucco wall, next to a chewed hamburger. Like most of the rats I encounter in print, it's a New York native, a Norway rat, also known as a brown rat, the bully of the rat world. In the Northeast and throughout the Midwest, they dominate, due to not only their size—a single rat can weigh four pounds—but also their sociability and frenetic reproduction. No matter the season or region, brown rats are known to fuck up to twenty times a day. One pair of lovers can produce 15,000 babies in a year. If they live a year. Brown rats must survive life on the streets.

As I read, I wait for an animal that resembles my own rat to scamper across the page. I scan the paragraphs for signs: split rinds, shredded petals, any mention of roofs. Like bullies everywhere, the brown rat crowds the page, edging out natural variety. When other rats do appear, they're often defined in comparison to the Norway rat. Consider the black rat, *rattus rattus*. The deuteragonist waiting in the rafters of the global rodent drama. Where the brown rat is big and bellicose, the black rat is "sleeker and smaller." It does not live down in the streets like the brown rat but in roofs and trees. It is "smarter" with "smoother fur" and "bigger ears." A "better climber." Yet, *Rattus rattus*, my rat, is not a star, not in the rat world, even as it sleeps closer than the rest to the moon.

When black rats arrived in California over 200 years ago, they fled a paradise lost. City by city, they were pushed out of the East Coast by the larger and more aggressive Norway rat. But they discovered a new paradise in the tousled palms and topiaries of Los Angeles. High in the foliage, black rats could build their nests in private. From the sidewalk, no human eye can discern their presence. If you encounter a black rat in the street, it's likely foraging for food. While black rats can eat almost anything, they prefer a vegetarian diet. At the Los Angeles Flower Mart, they seek carnation seeds. They feast on corsages. My jealousy peaks when I read that they can consume a whole bloom, nectar to pistil.

Last winter, LA's historic rat problem received national attention when deputy attorney Elizabeth Greenwood filed a $5 million suit against the city after she allegedly contracted typhus from an infected flea carried into her office by rats. "The rats have been there for decades," Greenwood told the press. "Everybody knows about it." The signs were, in fact, obvious: greasy streaks on the walls, paw prints on notepads, spilled pots, gnawed jack-o'-lanterns. Employees filed complaints about the infestation with the mayor's office. But the rats persisted.

LA's rat population may very well be exploding. Hard data is hard to find. According to local exterminators, however, the rat population changes little year to year. "Rats are animals of opportunity," says Louis Rico, owner of a Westside rat control company, in a recent interview with *LA Mag*. "The more lush your garden, the more food there is for rats."

Rattus rattus are now native Angelenos, and the City has used various strategies over the years to combat them. One creative solution is the Working Cats Program, initiated in 1999 to control the infestation at the Flower Mart downtown. Feral cats slated to be euthanized are sterilized, vaccinated, and relocated to homes and businesses across the city to control rat populations. In

2007 the Wilshire division of the Los Angeles Police Department began using cats in the parking lot outside the station. Soon officers no longer worried about rat sightings during smoke breaks.

Rats taste it all. Flowers *and* cigarettes. Their only sense more developed than taste is touch. According to biologists, rats are *thigmophilic*, or touch-loving. They prefer to touch things as they travel: walls, rails, corners. Especially corners. "Rats are thought to feel safest when they are simultaneously touching a wall and free to escape," writes Robert Sullivan in his book *Rats*. I circle the word "simultaneously." I'm almost charmed.

The romance of rat life. Pea shoots, stone fruit, honeysuckles, berries straight off the vine.

Hollowed oranges, pomelos, lemons and limes. Wild roses, star jasmine, raw tulips in the spring.

Out in the chaparral hills, before the ranch houses were built, rats cracked sunflower seeds against their teeth. When they left the shards behind, new stalks sprouted. A riot of yellow. Their hunger was useful: they spread the seeds of the flowers they devoured. Other times they gnawed off the reproductive parts of invasive weeds, stopping their creep across the canyon. They lived off the fat of the land, and once fat, they became even more useful as meals for hawks and snakes.

At the brewery by my apartment, I read about water rats at a picnic table in the sun. When my phone vibrates, it shakes the whole bench. I look at the screen, swipe to answer, *Hey mom!* She tells me she's driving home from the doctor. A pain in her hip. Her knee. A problem with her blood pressure. *I'm sleeping terribly*, she says. *Me too*, I tell her. *But you've always had trouble sleeping*, she says. The wind kicks up, I kill the last of my beer. *It's different*, I explain. *There's a rat living on my roof. At least I'm pretty sure it's a rat.* I watch a plastic bag dance by the taco truck. *Have you tried melatonin?* she asks. I let the silence hang between us. I try to think of a different topic. What I ate for lunch. My recent trip to the desert. I say nothing. She wants to know what I'm reading. I confess: *Mostly books about rats.* She says, *Aren't you researching those bars by that beach? Did you quit?* I'm unsure if she's asking a question or making a prediction so I laugh. I say, *Hold on.* The wind blows the napkins off the table. I run circles trying to gather them.

One quick lick to seal the seam of the blunt. It's what we do: sit on the carpet and watch the smoke rise. Window open. The sounds of the street mix with Mark's talk of fuzz pedals. The eternal crack of skateboards hitting the concrete, the roll. Somewhere, a couple is fighting. We can't make out the words, though they're yelling, louder than we ever did in our ten years together. The lighter flames blue, then yellow. When the record stops, I turn it over. In this way, Mark and I still enjoy each other.

But tonight Mark leaves the apartment, and I set the scene for seduction. Blanc de blancs in a paper cup. A candle in a tin. I strike the match and watch the wick struggle to catch. In the steaming tub, I blow bubbles off my stomach. The bathroom grows dark. These days the sun drops out of the sky, but the cold nights never come. The windows stay open all season. No Santa Anas to beat the leaves off the trees. The palms static on the hillside.

After my bath I put on a record. Alone, I let the music boom. The rat taps above my head. The sound of its movements fuse with my own so I hear only the bass, my heart, its feet. *Tap, tap, tap.* I turn the record louder still. A high-pitched guitar. Slowly, I start to dance, swaying my hips, arms stiff. I catch a glimpse of myself in the bathroom mirror: a wind-up doll jerking back to life. The scurrying stops. It runs again. As if in rhythm. I shake my arms loose, on the beat with my furry friend. I find myself almost believing the line I read this afternoon: rats dance.

I fall asleep liking the rat. And stay asleep. A miracle, a whole night of peace.

Another sign of seduction: I start paying attention to trash in the street. Not only the type of trash, or whether it is edible, but its volume, location, and meaning within the greater trash universe. A half-eaten lemon on my neighbor's lawn is a window into what happens when the sun sets. Crushed *Hot Cheetos* means kids are near. Empty beer cans in the blue bin outside the apartment door tells me Mark is inside with his friends. I walk on. I let the litter guide me, a Magic 8 Ball leading me through the dark streets and the dead weeks.

3. WAITING WITH THE BAR RATS

Spring – Summer 2019

I plan many visits back to the University of Irvine library. Sometimes I pay to park in the packed campus lot, then drive off without opening the car door. This surprises me every time. Because I'm here specifically to paw through the personal papers of Robert F. Gentry and other archives, to chart the evolution of southern Orange County from hippie heaven to conservative cliché.

I stumbled onto the area's bohemian past by accident, while researching another project about a local cult, Children of God, a religious group formed in Huntington Beach in the late sixties. My cult research was personal: my mom and father were members of the group in the 1980s.

For years, Children of God, and its charismatic leader, David Berg, obsessed me. I published a chapbook and several essays about the cult. Still, my curiosity mushroomed. Seasons piled up, my nose in a book, eyes affixed to the screen. I couldn't turn away from ex-members' stories of forced bible memorization, ceaseless migration, and sexual predation. Then, in one memoir, a passing line upended my obsession: "All the gays in Laguna Beach." *All the gays?* The author wrote the line as if it were common knowledge. I typed the phrase into my phone. Articles with titles like, "Historic Gay Bar Closing" burned on the screen. Spot after spot had shuttered, with only one queer bar left in all of Orange County. I kept reading, preferring to linger less and less on the violence of cultlife and more on the sticky dance floors with the gay bar rats.

Today, I blow off my session at the Irvine University Library again and drive South in search of those sticky floors. Today, I cruise straight through the city's heart, down to the coast, past the beach, into the canyon where the birds sing all day long, or so I read somewhere.

I decide that my new research method will be simple: visit every former gay bar in Laguna. I'll chart the demise of "Southern California's original gay beach" one converted dive at a time. My sole job: sit in the sun and drink. Research even a dead person can perform.

There are only two ways into Laguna Beach: Pacific Coast Highway and Laguna Canyon Road. I drive through the canyon, scanning the roadside for purple lupine. High above the city, I find only shuddering scrub. A view not unlike the one Gentry might've seen in 1970 when he moved to Laguna. Up here, it's easy to time travel. Among the lemon gum, I can imagine how the city looked in the

1970s or even the 1920s, before real estate developers and television producers reimagined it forever. I emerge from the canyon, descend into the city, and the version of Laguna I glimpsed on TV emerges: palms, peach condos, glass-walled houses high on the bluffs. Pale men in silk hibiscus shirts push strollers down shaded sidewalks. In the windows, canelés sleep on silver trays. There are oil paintings of lighthouses and wild horses. At the crosswalk, I wait beside a tall blonde woman in white jeans and a thin camisole. Her square pink nails are a shock against so much white. When she walks into the street, a group of teens call out to her. Everyone waves. I squint into the distance, trying to locate the ocean. To remind myself where I am.

The streets distract me. I watch the teens clot and scatter, their hair shiny and straight as their teeth. In between racks of macramé bikinis, I eat sunflower seeds, flip through ditzy dresses with puffy sleeves, peach and ivory. I pass a tie-dye parking meter, which upon closer inspection, is not a functioning meter but a cruel art installation called "Create Change, Don't Give Change." A tiny steel plate reads, "Help us keep our streets free of panhandlers, deposit loose change here." I imagine a red-faced homeowner standing before a crowded city council meeting, mouthing the words, *Art for a good cause!* Every meter I see dotting the city streets cheerfully announces, *The housing insecure are not welcome here!* I walk toward the water to rinse the image from my mind. I am looking for clues. Portals. I want to time travel, high in the canyon, but also here in the city center. How else will I find the one-time "epicenter of gay nightlife"? I walk on.

I crave the buzz of the hunt. The romance of research. Details, minor histories, shards of human experience. When I hold what's been lost or forgotten in my gaze, it feels like love.

On the patios, I'm searching for historical signposts to help me understand how this city, in the 1980s, at the height of a national conservative backlash, came to elect one of the first gay politicians. Perhaps because when Gentry was elected in 1982, the city was not yet home to the uber wealthy. I suspect that the city's transformation from gay mecca to bougie resort might be related to the AIDS crisis, which decimated the local gay community and made way for real estate redevelopment. Laguna's annual rate of new HIV cases in 1990 was 1.42 per 1,000 people; in San Francisco, which had the highest rate among major U.S. cities, it was 1.29. An estimated 25% of Laguna's 26,000 residents were gay. In the first five years of the epidemic, 184 cases of HIV or AIDS were reported and 119 Laguna residents died. A real estate boom followed.

AIDS in Laguna Beach was largely invisible to outsiders. Then as now. Today what remains to mark this forgotten history is a small volunteer-maintained garden memorial on the cliff behind the former Boom Boom Room, indistinguishable at first glance from other lookout points. There is a dedicated bench, prayer candles in pink and green glass, cement flip flops, a coffee mug glued to the dirt, a crown of feathers, loose beads, a plaque that reads, "The bars are gone but the memories of friends who lost their lives to AIDS remain." I want to know the stories behind the names.

The first bar I visit in Laguna is The Little Shrimp. It isn't the oldest gay bar in Laguna, nor the most beloved, but it may have the deepest history. After The Little Shrimp shuttered in 1995, the building, on the corner of Pacific Coast Highway and Cress, became home to a second, equally loved gay supper club called Woody's By the Beach. It was at these clubs that Gentry and his friends plotted political and environmental policies like preserving Laguna's beaches and stopping offshore drilling. Today, even Woody's has disappeared. Which doesn't deter me. I enter the bars' history like a rat. Sideways. Late. I sit on the patio of the modern Tex-Mex chain erected from their rubble and sniff for traces of the past. I watch the sun drop out of the sky. The wooden tables fill. When asked, I nod, *Another*. The cocktail gives me an ice cream headache. Today, no one on this patio looks gay. Not even me.

"When I can't write, I go in and play with the rat," writes Brenda Hillman, a poet who knows the differences between rats in the attic and rats in the barn, rats we pet and rats that trawl trash, rats that run mazes and rats that rule our dreams. Of these I prefer the ones that come to me while I sleep. How they edge out all other visitors. If I sleep.

I do try to write. I channel Hillman and Marguerite Duras. "I write as if I were already dead," Duras once said. Already dead, I open my notebook. I sit on a patio. I sit on a boardwalk. I let the notebook fill with sand. August burns into September. Every day I write my name and the date on the top of the page. I trace the numbers in blue ink.

Sleep continues to elude me. Even the rat seems to retire before me. Its movements cease at the pink crease of dawn. I rise. The sight of my face troubles me. I tape a large black and white photo of Marguerite Duras to the bottom of my bathroom mirror. When I look into the glass, her face stares back at me. Her big square glasses. The deep folds around her mouth. Her puffy eyes. She is sitting on the floor, on the set of her 1972 film *Jaune le soleil*. The face in this photo is different from the most famous version of her face, the one emblazoned on the cover of her most famous book, *The Lover*, shot when she was a beautiful young girl. I prefer her face as it looks in 1972. Witchy. This is what I tell myself. I prefer her ravaged.

When a red smudge appears across the top of the Duras

print, I admire the smooth texture of the lipstick and wonder what brand it is. That night I ask Mark if he's bringing lovers over without telling me. He says, *Nope.* The evidence says otherwise. I don't argue. I remember the rat runs above his room, too.

It hasn't rained in months, but the grass outside the Coast Inn is crayon green. The plants look plastic. I don't find them any less beautiful. From outside, it's impossible to tell this building once housed the Boom Boom Room, the famous gay disco on the coast.

If I had one hundred and seventy five dollars in my bank account tonight, I could unlock the white door of a room at the Coast Inn. I could tell you if the pillows on the bed have flowers or stripes, if the AC is a box in the window or a dusty vent on the wall. Selfie in the mirror. Flash on. Tonight there are sixty eight dollars in my bank account. So I leave the car parked along the highway and snoop around in the clipped green grass.

I push past the banana leaves. The gate is locked. I don't rattle the handle. I wait for a guest to come and punch the code into the metal ring. The gate is painted the same streaky white as the doors of every room. An upturned chaise faces the ocean, an ashtray filled with liquid. When a shirtless man in flip flops opens the sliding glass door to his balcony, smoke pours from his mouth. The windows of the lobby are dark. The Inn is no longer even an inn but an Airbnb. In front of the main building, where guests can check in and out without encountering another person, sits a squat brick building with a low brown roof and windows papered over with grainy prints of a beach at sunset. This was once the "The Boom," as some local patrons called it.

Below the bluff, girls in tie-dye bikinis rush into the water one by one. They shriek. A wide, sandy cove, West Beach is the only gay beach in Orange County. In 1968, when the City of Laguna purchased Main Beach and turned it into a public park, the gay community who called Main Beach home moved West down the coast. The bars followed. High on the hill, the lit windows of the Boom Boom Room gleamed, and around the corner, at the cabaret, a queen played piano in a silk dress, a sequined jumpsuit, a gold lamé gown, an onyx cigarette holder between her lips. Down the street, smoke coated the windows inside the Little Shrimp, turning the blue waves outside purple. I can almost see the smoke rings, standing here in the shade of the Boom Boom Room's low brown roof. The violet waves. The lit fish tank that Rock Hudson leans against to light a Camel. Bette Midler is in the corner, her hair, a red mist rising above the disco lights. I want to inhale everything. Paul Lynde spilling vodka in the blue light, head tilted back in laughter.

In the 1973 animated film version of *Charlotte's Web*, Paul Lynde voices Templeton, a rat who lives beneath the trough of a sad pig. When Wilbur the pig arrives at Zuckerman's farm, he has no friends and spends his days crying in the hay. But he knows what he wants. "Love," writes E.B. White. Templeton's pleasures are less lofty: cold leftovers, gossip, and long visits to the dump. "I prefer to spend my time spying and hiding," he says. Also collecting: seeds, straw, shotgun shells. He possesses no shame. He is greedy and curious. A special breed of fun.

As a child, my obsession with *Charlotte's Web*, whose central theme is the inevitability of death, worried my mother. My father passed away when I was two, and she believed I identified with Wilbur and his delusional quest to forestall his death through friendship and dazzling language. What she didn't know was that Wilbur's hopefulness annoyed me. It would take me years, in fact, to find value in Wilbur and his tears. Back then I skipped his scenes to glut with Templeton at the fair.

The fair is a veritable smorgasbord, sings Templeton, sliding under its gates. A psychedelic smorgasbord. The night awash in green light. Goodies everywhere. He dances in the glare of a Ferris wheel. He eats. He tastes it all. Melon rinds, moldy pie, greasy paper bags stuffed with rotten eggs. With a piece of Swiss cheese looped on his tail, he skates across double-ring barrels and abandoned picnic tables, his stomach so swollen it swings. He sings on the way back to the farm: *Each night, when the lights go out, it can be found, on the ground, all around.*

When I imagine what it might've been like to party as an openly gay man in Southern California in the 1970s, I imagine Templeton's fair scene. A smorgasbord of bodies, powders, bottles, bathrooms where I can unzip a stranger's jeans. In my dream, I'm Templeton rooting through the night with my mouth, awash in red lights. I dance. I eat. I taste. Through the window, a spray of black waves. The Pacific is a small square compared to the expanse of my body. Every pore an orifice.

Most of the gay history I encounter in books like Samuel R. Delaney's *Times Square Red, Times Square Blue* and Scotty Bower's *Full Service* foregrounds the experiences of the urban gay man. Often these men enjoyed regular access to consensual sex through bars, bathhouses, theaters, and cruising. Envy and desire bloom when I read about a lavish 800-person party at the Inn that lasted three days. A scene I could only imagine happening in a city. It was uncommon for me to read about queers who milked cows, or lived anywhere near a barn, much less a rat-filled pasture. Even Templeton must flee the farm to live what he calls the "high life."

My high life: reading all morning and through the night. I wake and do it again. It is the only good reason I can find sometimes to brew the coffee, open the blinds, let the light in.

Today, the afternoon burns up as I read on a red towel at the beach with 1,000 steps. The sky is milky gray and puffy as my face. No one bothers swimming in this weather. I dawdle in the sand, out past the punks, tide rising. I watch them vape in the waning light, throw rocks into a cave. There are belts of brown kelp black with flies. I stay until the tide forces me to leave. I drive home slow. Driving soothes me. Between the yellow lines, I'm contained. The confusion of the side streets gives way to the thrill of the merge, the numb harmony of the freeway. Each lane the same as the others. My hours defined by blurry lines.

My first year in California I drove over 100 miles a day. I was no Easy Rider: often I ended where I began. I was a grad student cutting through suburbs shadowed by rollercoasters. I was a weed delivery girl, weighing out bags in cul-de-sacs. I was a private tutor. A nanny who crisscrossed the valley. For many years, these commutes were all I knew of the city.

Now, when I can't use Mark's car, I ride the bus. My route has a romantic name: the Silver Line. On it I ride from San Pedro to Pershing Square, and from there to Hollywood or Santa Monica, any place named in a pop song. Two, three hours ass-flat in the scooped seat. My breath wet against the window. A white vignette framing the city. It feels so good to look so long out the window.

Just look. A real, ripe pleasure. To be a passenger in life.

Wasted days and wasted nights, I sing from the passenger's seat, wind snuffing my voice. Rachel drives us east towards the Mojave Desert. Since we met two months ago at the ramen shop, we've seen each other nearly every weekend, often getting together to read in the park or nerd out on self-guided walking tours of historical architecture. Now, as we cruise past Palmdale, I speak faster and faster, telling Rachel about today's destination, an abandoned socialist colony in the heart of the Antelope Valley, where little grows but wildflowers and sagebrush. Waste is on our minds today. Ruins and rebirth. Rachel is still writing her dissertation, a project about failure. Specifically, building materials that suicide over time. Clay bricks that expand and crack. Hardwood that warps. *Screws tell stories,* she says over the steel guitar. Trash cans and bollards. A rock hits her windshield as we crest over the burned hills. *How's the rock changed by its flight?* she asks.

Flat panes of brown rush past the dash. Stinky creosote out the window. Exhaust and pesticides mix with my cigarette smoke, and I inhale deep. I tell her about the Nordic architect who dreamed that ancient ruins would one day come to life and flee the societies that now oppress them. *Tell me more,* she says. But we've already arrived. She sees the ruins for herself.

In the distance a brick grid and two crumbling fireplaces frame a cell tower. These are the ruins of Llano del Rio, all that remains of a once-thriving socialist colony built before Hollywood. Telephone poles rise from the mesquite. Rusted cans, crushed glass dot the sand. *Nowhere California* is spray-painted on the sidewall of a concrete pit filled with bottle caps. A rat's nest is felted between two rocks.

The sun is sharp, lashing Rachel's face with shadows. She trails the cracked bricks with her fingers, feeling for signs of revolt. Behind a clump of greasewood, I squat to pee. Once I read that human urine is good for soil, a solid source of nitrogen and potassium. I let rip.

On a warm stone, I sit and watch big black birds drop down and hang in the air. I'm nostalgic for a time when it seemed possible to revolutionize society simply by fleeing the city, holing up in the desert with friends. I want to believe in utopia. But my last trip to the desert with friends nearly killed me. A truck full of sweet onions honks.

The earliest residents of Llano del Rio may have been friends when they pitched their tents on that dusty strip on May Day 1914, the colony's official launch date. But by 1918 most of the 1,100 colonists had left. The California Commissioner of Corporations had denied Llano's application to build a dam to irrigate their land and sued the colony's founder, Job Harriman, for improper use of local water supplies. Harriman and two hundred loyal Llanoites soon fled to western Louisiana where there was no shortage of rivers or rain. In both California and Louisiana, Llano admitted only whites.

When we think of communal experiments, we imagine failure. "The dream of an alternative way of being is…dismissed as naive, simplistic, or a blatant misunderstanding of the nature of power in modernity," writes Jack Halberstam in *The Queer Art of Failure*. This is especially the case with utopian communities, communes, and cooperative colonies, which after the 1960s are tainted by their association with media stereotypes of the hippie counterculture, a bunch of half-baked longhairs stringing beads, cruising out on LSD, and waxing their asses with insincere Hare Krishnas. But like utopian writer Aldous Huxley, I believe failed experiments are valuable *as failures*. Our collective failures add to our knowledge of the most important of all art forms – the art of living together.

Despite the explosion of documentaries and podcasts devoted to free love communes and death cults, one rarely hears about California's many utopian communities, but their impact is felt today. One can find traces of Llano's architectural radicalism in Orange County's own utopia: Disneyland.

Architect Alice Constance Austin's designs for Llano featured a radial plan, kitchenless houses, and an elaborate network of utility tunnels. In her vision, kitchens were centralized. Food was prepared communally and delivered to individual houses through a network of rail tunnels, which would also transport laundry and trash. Inspired by British architect Ebenezer Howard's "garden apartments," Austin's plans eliminated private housework and provided a model for both affordable housing and the necessary infrastructure to make cooperative living possible on an urban scale. "The Socialist city should be beautiful," she wrote in her notes. Tunnels, she believed, were essential to preserving the tranquility of the city streets.

Walt Disney agreed. In designing Disney's ideal city in Anaheim, his team used a circular plan similar to Austin's designs, complete with an extensive underground tunnel system that allowed workers to move through the park unseen by guests.

Every night when the gates close, hundreds of custodians, landscapers, and set designers emerge to tend Disneyland's eighty-five-acre grounds after a day of abuse by visitors. They scrape gum from under table tops. Scrub saliva from glass surfaces. Dust, mist, and trim the plants. With the crowds gone, the park's resident cats also come out to work.

No one knows when the cats arrived at the park, but sightings date back to the mid-1950s. As with the Working Cats Program, the two hundred or so felines who live at Disneyland are spayed and neutered and receive food and basic medical care but are otherwise left alone to sleep and slink among the park's 100,000 plus trees and shrubs. At night they earn their keep by stalking the park's most loyal guests: rats.

Low sun. I walk past shaggy hibiscus flowers, down the hill, towards the beach. *Where's mine,* a man calls out the window of his parked truck. *Hey you,* he says. *Hey, HEY.* My eyes scan for his license plate, which reads *1 MORE X.* In the passenger's seat, a dog is barking at a squirrel on the sidewalk. The man says, *Stop it.* His hands disappear into the dog's fur. My breathing doesn't slow until I see the fire pits, the wedge of sand.

But at home, in bed, I no longer tremble at the first *scratch, scratch, scratch* of the night. Just slip on my headphones, lean back into the pillows. Every hour or so I push the headphones off and check if the rat is gnawing. Last week I read that rats' teeth grow constantly. To keep their incisors from puncturing their skulls, they must spend hours grinding their teeth against each other. Still, I think it can't go on every time I slip the headphones off.

It goes on.

2,181 miles away in Georgia, my Mom confronts her own pests. *Roaches in the rain gutter,* she says over the phone. I'm at the beach, and the tide is high. I stick to the sand banks. *Mold dots on the walls when it rains,* she says. *Do you want to see a picture?* The shot is a blurry white wall. I squint at the photo, searching for signs of moisture. I realize I can't remember the last time I saw rain. *Jealous of your storms*, I say. *I miss mushrooms and big yellow boots.*

Pursy, the mushrooms that grow under the porch of Mom's new apartment in my sister's backyard, a bachelor studio with a fridge, two windows, and a single person shower. It's not ideal, the arrangement my mom has with my sister and her husband. Mom receives affordable housing, and my sister receives affordable childcare, but they have to live together, forever. *I can't get them to repair anything*, mom tells me, as if the landlords are strangers. I want to ask her if she's sad that she no longer lives in the house with the kids, if her new spot in the backyard feels as far away from my sister's house as California from Georgia. But I say *Jealous. A cheap place to stay.* Then, I rip a big laugh as if I'm joking.

For others it's different, but I never tire of living by the ocean, the slip of blue at the bottom of a dead end street, pressing my body flat against the guard rail, cresting in the sun, high above the crush of sand, bodies, foam. I find myself searching for these dead ends everywhere I go. Those bright instances of flight.

My library sits on a cliff overlooking the sea. As I shelve books, I see patches of blue through the breaks in the trees. The pollen makes me sneeze all afternoon. Ragweed and oak. Box elders by the fountain. When I walk outside, my eyes itch. Loose bougainvillea blooms spangle the sidewalk, making it slippery. Banana leaves frame the path down to the street where the main book-drop sits under a spray of palms. Their short, tidy skirts *sssss* in the breeze. The sun sinks into the cove. I toss bestsellers with glossy covers into a black cloth cart then push it back up the path to the library basement. When I click on the light, two fat rats run past me out the door into the banana trees. I scream. My voice rings through the old stone building. My coworker rounds the basement corner and I say, *I'm fine. I saw a rat.* He laughs and asks, *That's it? I'll call facilities.* His body betrays no signs of fear as he charges upstairs. He says into the receiver: *Small problem.* I stay in the basement, door wide open, trying to slow my pulse.

A week later two men in blue jumpsuits install compact black boxes that look like electric enclosures along the outside walls of the library. The men come back the following afternoon to check the traps. *Chockablock*, they tell us. My skin prickles. Soon I start noticing the same black boxes outside the grocery store at the end of my street. I find them by the wall of my hair salon, gym, and pizza shop. The whole city chockablock. The idea both frightens and delights me. I ask my coworker, *Did you know rats can laugh?* He shakes his head, *No.*

On the Fourth of July I catch a ride to Santa Ana to drink warm beer and watch fireworks with Jess. She's a new friend, and she wants me to tour her pink duplex and its green, green yard. It's late afternoon when I arrive, but already the teens next door are setting off Lady Fingers. They high-five each other each time one goes BOOM. *I like the ones that pop like champagne*, Jess says.

The sky a bruised peach. I take a picture of her putting on lipstick in the reflection of a silver 12 oz. can. A row of motionless palms. At dusk the other neighbors come outside and fire their own rockets and flares. The beer makes me flash a big dumb smile whenever I look at the lit sky. When I turn away, I'm sad again. Why does exploding shit feel like a triumph? BOOM. I smile at the fake stars and the real ones too.

Home from the party, and I can't sleep. I thumb through the photographer Hal Fischer's book *The Gay Seventies*, lingering over the black-and-white street-style shots taken between 1972 and 1978. A jolt of borrowed nostalgia. On one page, "Basic Gay" captions a frame of a man in cuffed jeans, Converse sneakers, and a checked shirt. The basic gay is mugging for the camera. Chin lifted, thumbs in his belt loops. In another shot, titled "Hippie," a man with long hair and an open smile wears suspenders and a sash. There are folly bells attached to his pants pockets. Each photo in the *Street Fashion* series is composed in more or less the same way: a man stands against a bare wall, thoroughly posed, direct eye contact with the camera. No pretense of spontaneity, authenticity of a moment. There is nothing casual about leather chaps in the shade, one hip cocked, or hands shoved in denim pockets. I want to glory forever in the brave raised chin, eyes straight into the lens.

Red towel spread. Sand in my hair. In the shade of a rock at West Street Beach I read about the gay dives. At the Boom Boom Room, men sniff nitrites in sepia light. I admit: I like to watch. I'm always looking.

I fall asleep, dream about brick-laying rats wearing hardhats. When I wake, the rock is no longer blocking the sun and my skin is red as my towel. I shake away the sand. On my phone, a string of missed texts from Mark. *Can you come home early? I need the car tonight. You ok?* The car's AC cools my sunburn. I text Mark, *On the way.* But I brake outside the Main Street Bar & Cabaret. The last gay bar operating in Laguna.

I find plenty of parking on the street. I feed the meter a dime, and it buys me four minutes. On the door, there is a gold crown painted above a peephole. A red and blue crest with a lion. On the sidewalk, I snap pictures of the cute brown shutters, the freshly painted wooden sign out front, twin pride flags marking the entrance. My meter blinks green to red. In the car, I start a group text thread with Rachel and Jess: *No one is here, but we should be.* My phone vibrates. Rachel asks, *When?* But I'm already on the freeway. I leave her message on read.

At the apartment, I cook rice and beans. In the sink, I find a strand of long blonde hair and wipe it away with my bare hand. I take a cold shower. When I remember to text Rachel back, it's past midnight. *Tomorrow*, I tell myself. *Later*. But I suspect I won't return to the Cabaret any time soon. I write in my journal: *I prefer the bars in my books to the bars I can sit in myself. Fantasy trumps reality every time.*

I rip out the page and begin again.

4. RATTING AFTER MIDNIGHT

It's the first day of November, and I light the pilot on the heater. On the TV, a woman tells me how I can hold joy. I picture it sitting in my palm like a fat California orange. *Quash your illusions about yourself and the world*, she says. I want to believe her. The promise of disillusioned joy. I want to pilfer her confidence. Walk into the day sure I can sniff my way out of any fool's paradise.

Driving through south Orange County, Rachel finds no paradise. She's in hell. A wash of outdoor shopping centers and mixed-use condos. Scant trees. As we near the university, my skin grows itchy. I want to finally walk through the doors of the Irvine Library, thumb the Gentry papers. I thought that with a friend I could. But I'm swamped with the same fear I feel whenever I near the campus: if I sit still in the silent library, I'll discover exactly how behind I've fallen since the trip to the desert with my friends. But if I delay entrance, I can ride the crest of possibility a little longer. The possibility of discovery. I turn to Rachel and say, *Let's stop. I'll show you something.* Rachel is sober so the bars offer me no escape today. I open my phone and load a map of Modjeska Canyon, in the Santa Ana Mountains outside Irvine. She zooms in on our new destination. *There's nothing there,* she says. I don't tell her this is the point. *It's the site of another failed commune,* I say. She asks, *Like Llano del Rio?* I say, *Sort of.* She wrinkles her forehead and looks out the window: *Here?* A fan of the TV show *The Real Housewives of Orange County,* she imagines the area as a sea of blond hair, cartoon boobs, and blue infinity pools. Our drive through Irvine does little to convince her otherwise. We pass by rows and rows of boxy houses with evergreen lawns secured by gates and hedges. *This place makes me nervous,* she says. *So much beige.*

This landscape, like much of Orange County, resembles the Orlando suburb where Rachel grew up. *When I was a kid, there were orange groves,* she says. *Now it's parking lots.* I don't tell her I see little difference between industrial citrus and industrial shopping. Coming from a rural Georgia town, with no malls or big box retailers, I still sense promise in all that tarmac. I can't let go of the fantasy that it's really possible to pave over my past.

A few turns and we're on a two-lane road in the canyon, blue jays and a big red maple. We pull over to the side of the blacktop and tramp through the dandelion weeds. No plaques mark the commune. No signs bear the name The Brotherhood of Eternal Love. The Brotherhood was not a bona fide commune. Nor were they a cult. They were essentially glorified drug dealers, but they proselytized like devout believers. Their religion? Lysergic acid diethylamide.

The story goes like this: in 1966 the founding members of the Brotherhood moved to Modjeska Canyon to live together among the laurel trees, manufacture their own acid (later called Orange Sunshine), and strategize how to spread the good word. To Brotherhood founder John Griggs, LSD had revolutionary potential. In his mind, the drug possessed unparalleled healing properties that allowed humans to see how they were inextricably connected to every living organism. In the early days, the Brotherhood often gifted their product. If humans could discover the inherent unity of the universe, a utopian society might manifest right here, right now.

On the drive home, Rachel imagines a different ending to the Brotherhood's story. In her version, they don't move to Laguna to open a head shop where longhairs flock. They don't become the "hippie mafia," an international drug smuggling team. They stay in the Canyon. They bake bricks in the sun, grow wild arugula. In my version, they smoke weed every day, eat fruit and fuck, discover the world through licking, as rats do. But when I start to say it out loud to Rachel, it sounds like another California dream, all vibes, no vexations.

In essays about Orange County, Modjeska Canyon is rarely mentioned. If one consults TV, it's possible to believe Orange County is devoid of nature altogether. "One box amidst a landscape of seemingly endless boxes," as one writer recently put it. "A place without history." As if it were possible to bulldoze our memories.

What does it mean for a place or a person to be without a history? What does it mean for us to want this fantasy?

Some people describe Orange County as a colorless, cultureless expanse of white silicone faces and clipped green lawns. They've never sat in the crabgrass outside Jess's pink duplex in Santa Ana eating a hoagie at dusk, watching the rats run.

Meatballs or bust, I tell Rachel. Late afternoon now. We wait in line at the sandwich shop with the winking bee out front. Inside, longshoremen scroll on their phones, chew through heroes thicker and longer than their forearms. When we get to the counter, she orders a cheese and avocado. We pay and walk to the park on top of the bluff, roll out our jackets in the grass. I eat my sandwich in one quick burst. She peels back one corner of her sub's wrapper. She takes a bite, reads her book, takes a bite.

In the grass two men kick a soccer ball. The clouds break, and the sun makes everyone sweat. I lie on my back in the weeds, hike my skirt around my thighs, let my skin absorb the heat. On my phone, I skim work emails, screen dimmed. I roll over on my stomach to ask Rachel when she wants to leave. She says, *Never*. I laugh. *Ha ha*. She leans over and kisses my chapped lips. I pull away, stunned. The shock soon gives way to pride. She can't tell I'm dead. Ha ha.

We're friends, I tell her. *Okay?* She stares ahead: *Sure.* But her face is tight, mouth downturned, the entire walk back to the car.

Back home, on the living room floor, eyes red, a text from Rachel shakes my phone. *I need space,* the message reads. I stare at the screen. It falls dark. I touch it back to life. *Greed is a vice,* Mark says, eyeing the joint in my hand. *Sorry,* I say. *I don't know how to respond to THIS.* He leans close. I hand him my phone. One thing I know: I don't want his advice. But here he is, next to me on the flat gray carpet. *Tell her you understand,* he says. *You respect her boundaries.* I type it out word for word.

Rachel was right to think I might desire her. Like Mark, she is nerdy. In her rumpled-collar shirts and baggy cable-knit sweaters, she looks like she walked off the set of a 1980s drama set at a college in New England. *It's charming, the way she talks of books as if they were her friend,* I write in my diary later that night. *I'm no longer sure what I want.*

People tell me rats are as scared of us as we are of them. But I have seen them charge into the night without compunction. No discernible hesitation. As if it's possible to know every contour of the darkness ahead.

If the common rat is as scared as me, let me leech its bravado.

Let me. Let me. Let me. Let me. Let me. Let me.

On Twitter, I watch a video of a rat falling from the ceiling at a Chipotle in Dallas. A large furry ball drops from the rafters onto a black rubber mat. Patrons photograph its supine body, its legs sticking straight in the air. The rat is stunned, motionless. Then it gets up and walks off.

Sometimes the rat doesn't walk away. I find one paralyzed in the street outside the library, its chest sunk, red line out its mouth. My coworker takes pictures of its dead body from different angles to send to facilities. The clicking of her phone upsets me. When she walks back inside, I'm alone with the rat. I cover it with a thick banana leaf I pull from a tree along the path. I scatter bougainvillea petals around its body.

I was not exactly alive the night I pitched my tent next to the sandstone boulders. A breakup with a new lover, a rebound relationship, still fresh, had drained me. I had hoped the blue pills and pulsing stars would revive me, remind me of essential truths, the vastness of the cosmos or whatever. I offered to share my drugs with Mark and Sean. They said *no*. I would go it alone. But I woke to the owls and the slow *shhhh* of the tent zipper. Mark's ratlike face hovering over me, his hand in my pants. I said, *It's you!* Surprised to realize I was no longer hallucinating. In the morning, my friends and I prepared breakfast on a wooden table with a beige cloth. Mark handed me a bowl of oatmeal and said, *Be careful it's hot.*

In the Lifetime movies I devoured as a kid, memories of sexual assault intrude as flashbacks. In the months after my assault, I experienced no such phenomenon. My memory needed no aids. I saw his face every day.

At my apartment, I watch him plug in his amp and play another take of "Don't Worry, Baby" with his bandmates. In the courtyard, they sip home brew and smoke fair-trade weed, eat barbacoa tacos. Around this time, in my diary, I start referring to my apartment as Persephone's Lair.

The Greek goddess Persephone dies for the first time when Hades kidnaps and detains her in Hell after watching her pick flowers in a meadow. Even once her mother, Demeter, helps her escape his grip, she's not free. "After tasting the fruit of the Underworld, Persephone is required to be a part-time resident of hell," writes Myriam Gurba, in an essay detailing the specific torture of seeing one's assailant thrive on a stage, in a classroom, at the bar, while you smile and dance and die inside.

Mark doesn't deny the reality of the assault. He does not deny who unzipped my tent and crawled inside. He simply believes this particular event has nothing to do with his day to day life.

One day, I ask Mark if it might be possible for him to not enter my room at night. Even if he needs to use the bathroom. I tell him, *I'm not afraid of you. I just want some privacy.* My request is as absurd as it is logical. *I'm embracing paradox*, I say, over and over, hands hitched on my hips. He says, *Makes sense.* Weeks later I remind him about our chat. *I'm trying*, he says. I don't know how to respond.

Sometimes I still sweat at the sound of Mark's voice when he asks, *How was your day?* He hands me a *LaCroix* and says, *It takes time to heal.* This is how his memory works. The past is always the past, and the future is far off, too far off to trifle with today. An easy enough story to believe.

My dancing shoes are white high-tops. I wear them when I start going out at night. The blue hour. When the rats wake. How else will I find out what I want? I set rules for myself. The most important: say yes to everyone who asks me out on the apps. Tonight she picks a karaoke bar downtown, but it could be the pinball dive next door, or the falafel shop around the corner where I ate lamb two nights ago on a different date. I follow her down the sidewalk, her fake leather jacket crunching loud as leaves. In the alley she talks about rock climbing, and I pretend to ignore the two black trash bags shuddering against a brick wall as if blown by the wind. I suspect rats. I say nothing.

Pizza in the park under a raft of old-growth palms. Their skirts shake, but the fronds are still. There is no wind. He doesn't seem to notice the palms, or any of the obvious clues in the grass. I feel a shot of pride when I notice details my dates miss. A private joy. I start finding rats everywhere I go. Signs of life. She texts me: *The moon tonight is huge!* So I take the bus to the banks of the LA River where I feed her Swedish Fish and try to hide my delight when I spy black streaks of fur cutting through the moss. Other times, I wait and wait, and she, he, they, never walk through the door. I vape alone in the parking lot, car idling by the dumpster, excited as I want, just me, when I see a rat tail shaking in the ivy.

It's possible to go out every night at dusk and walk down every alley in the city and never glimpse one living rat. To the untrained eye, signs aren't signs. Fallen fruit is fallen fruit. Trash is trash. Ratting is another way of paying attention.

In the mornings, the rat is silent. I wake slow, cook sweet potatoes. The sun whites out every surface in the room. My phone tells me I should be at brunch, but I'm in bed, reading a story called "An Aesthetics of Rat Bites." A tribute to the beauty of those rosy welts that "present themselves in clusters, not so much organization as orgiastic," in the words of the author. In the city where the narrator lives, rats are so numerous that locals have learned to admire the bites. I find myself looking for clues as to what kind of rat is doing the biting. "They are communal, travel in packs," the narrator tells us. "Their nests seethe." *Not my rat!* I say. But maybe I'll learn something new. I read on. Which kind of rat leaves orgiastic bites? Blushed birthmarks? Scalded little welts? I let myself go.

Dates sometimes ask me about my living situation. *Very European*, I say. Mostly, though, I avoid bringing anyone home. Even if Mark leaves for the weekend. In truth, I fear becoming "the rat girl" in stories those lovers might share with their friends over eggs Benedict. I console myself with facts: black rats rarely live longer than 12 months. I can wait it out.

Sometimes I fantasize about moving down the street, across the country, far, far away. Nevada. Oklahoma. The Florida Keys. There I would sweat out toxins in my own studio, complete with avocado green tiles in the bathroom and a lemon tree in the yard. All mine.

The first decent apartment I see on Zillow has no fruit trees on the lawn, no lawn at all. The pictures show a concrete courtyard with two metal picnic tables. The apartment boasts new carpets and a shower resembling an upturned coffin, all mine for $1,800 a month. It's located three miles from the library and two miles from a strip of ocean locals call RAT Beach, which I learn from the ad. *No pets*, it says. *All applicants must show proof of income 3x the rent.* I throw my phone across the bed.

I'm searching for a new place to live, I find myself telling Mom a few days later on FaceTime. *Me too,* she says. *You know the Villa Palazzo?* I do not know the Villa Palazzo. I imagine billowy oak trees dotting the lawn, grape vines painted on rustic plates. *Where dreams come true?* I ask her. I'm two glasses into a bottle of red and can see a ring of rust forming around my lips. *Huh?* she says. I try again: *Is it a condo? A duplex?* She sends me a link to a senior living facility for independent elders. *24/7 service,* she says. *Montessori inspired memory care.* As I soon discover, this is a cutting-edge treatment for dementia patients. *Is your memory failing you?* I ask. *Not nearly enough,* she tells me.

Later I dream I'm on a gondola steered by a black rat wearing a beret. We float under brick bridges and past apartment buildings with clothing lines strung beneath them. We bob by factories then fields, green and brown. I start to recognize specific hay bales. I see the same red sweaters on the lines over and over. I ask the captain, *What kind of tour is this?* The captain doesn't understand me. He only speaks rat. I lay back in the boat and eat chunks of ciabatta from a woven sack. When I look up, the captain rat is gone. A goose drives the boat past a familiar field.

I wake and blame the word *palazzo* for the gondola ride that never ends. My mouth is dry, and my teeth feel fuzzy from the wine. I can't find my phone in the sheets. When I do, I don't like what it tells me. *2:36 a.m.* The street is quiet. My room is quiet, too, save for the rat running above my head.

Haloed in blue light, I read about Villa Palazzo on my phone. Mom is touring the facility next week. I zoom in on a picture of the grounds. The trees that line the drive are hyper-saturated as if dyed green. I lower the brightness on my screen. I discover that Villa Palazzo is Here to Serve. They offer yoga, restaurant-style dining, a movie theater, and a bar as well as off-site transportation, pet services, and memory care. I cannot find the cost of the rent. There are no prices on the Villa Palazzo website. There are green buttons that say *Contact Us*.

On Seniorly.com, an outside aggregator of senior care services, I learn that a private suite at Villa Palazzo costs an estimated $4,000 a month, or more than four times what mom can afford. I click play on a video tour of Villa Palazzo and its mulch courtyards. A woman laughs with a towel on her head at an on-site hair salon. A woman laughs while driving a waxed golf cart. A woman laughs while drinking red wine with friends by a stone fire pit.

I feel closer to my mom tonight than I have in weeks.

I sometimes fantasize about other things than fleeing. Like killing the rat. One day I dial my building's maintenance line, only to hang up on the first ring. The number calls me back. I speak slowly into the receiver: *Clogged shower. Slow drain. But I think I can fix it myself after all.*

Outside a restaurant, I eat lo mein in the car and watch the parking lot fill. My fortune cookie reads: *Stop searching forever, happiness is next to you.* The sentiment annoys me. What is happiness without the romance of the search?

December charges in, fog on the hills. The tankers move slow in the harbor. I know it's really winter when the snails line up along the sill. The ants move inside. So do the crickets and the rats. I listen for them. Deep in Ratlandia, I'm no longer interested exclusively in *Rattus rattus* but in all rat varieties, all over the city. Fortunately for me, LA is now the second rattiest city in the country.

While the infestation at city hall is old news, city officials have developed a new explanation: the unhoused population living downtown. Representative of this view is Deputy Attorney Elizabeth Greenwood who, in an interview with *The Daily Breeze,* urged city officials to address the infestation and "move the homeless people." According to the *Los Angeles Times*, the city's recent 12% rise in homelessness is "fueling speculation of a growing public health crisis of rats and trash near homeless encampments."

Fueling speculation also might be the *LA Times* itself, which has published over ten articles between April and August 2019 explicitly linking the city's historic rat problem with the current homeless crisis.

In the months before the *LA Times'* surge in rat reporting, the city council voted to allow homeless residents living in certain areas, like Skid Row, to sleep on the street and keep their possessions with them. Meaning: police sweeps of encampments in key downtown areas were no longer legal. Meaning: the city's once-abstract homeless crisis became increasingly concrete and visible to anyone traveling downtown.

As I thumb through the news reports of rats invading the city, I think of Katharina Fritsch's sculpture *Rattenkönig*, or *Rat King*, a circle of 16 towering rats knotted together by their tails. In German folklore, the rat king was seen as a bad omen, most likely due to rats' collective reputation as carriers of disease, as in the tale of the *Pied Piper of Hamelin*. In Fritsch's piece, my instinctual fear of rats is manifested, and it takes up physical space in a room, dominating it. At nine feet tall, the black acrylic rats seem impenetrable, like the myth of the rat king itself.

What do we miss when we write about rats as mythic animals of doom and disease and nothing else? When we portray rats as dirty outsiders? Like Fritsch's acrylic beasts, the myth of the rat looms large, blocks all else from view.

But if we look past the hulking facade of the rat, a more complicated picture emerges. Prolonged drought and increased land development in LA county has led to habitat destruction. Rats cannot invade our city. The city is already theirs.

I'm smoking on the roof when it finally happens: I see my rat for the first time sliding down an electrical wire. I glimpse its beefy body midair and my shoulders tense. It looks exactly as I imagined. Dark brown fur, almost black, long tail. My fear surprises me. I prefer to believe I can overpower my instincts. *Relax*, I tell myself. *You like rats. You find them charming.* The rat sprints across the ledge, down the drainpipe into the fog. In my mind, I wave au revoir to it. On the roof, in real time, I gasp.

5. YEAR OF THE RAT

Winter 2020

Late January. I find gray rat faces spray-painted on the sidewalks of my neighborhood. They feel like a message from the universe. In the Chinese zodiac, 2020 marks the Year of the Rat. A sign of wealth and surplus for those born under its sign, the rat is associated with the hour before and after midnight and symbolizes the beginning of a new day.

I meet Heidi on the apps. She lives in San Francisco but flies to LA every other week for work. I know I like her when I tell her I'm writing about rats, and she says, *There's plenty in my backyard. Want to see?*

When the roof rat goes, I hardly notice it. I so thoroughly trained myself to ignore the rat that its actual absence doesn't immediately register. Until it does. Leveled in bed with a migraine, I sweat out the night. A cold washcloth over my eyes. Mark turns on the kitchen tap. The water hits the metal sides of the sink and sounds like a car crash. I hear the front door open and close. The lock snaps into place. I'm alone, and the apartment is quiet. Too quiet. I check the time. Eleven pm. The hour of the rat. I hear nothing. Night after night, I listen. Close my eyes, crane my neck, stand on my bed, stretch toward the ceiling. Nothing.

Heidi sends me a different soundtrack. A song from a band called Ratboys. A narrated video of the split oranges on her lawn.

Soon gray cat faces start appearing on sidewalks and the sides of cars. In the mailroom, a neighbor tells me they saw some teens spray painting whiskers on a tree trunk the other night.

I possess no direct connection to the universe.

Maybe the message is: a new day. If you want.

I drive to her hotel in Marina del Rey. In the elevator, a big wet kiss against mirrored walls. Spilled cream on white sheets. Spilled coffee in the morning. Her face, haloed in the milky yellow light of a lamp bolted to the nightstand. I drive the same way every time she flies into LAX. I line my lips in the elevator. I dance across our hotel room to a slow country burn.

The hotel bed has white pillows, white sheets, and a white duvet. I lie down on the bed as if casting myself on a screen. A blank space where I can imagine and reimagine myself as anything.

I wait for Heidi at a bar in a strip mall near her hotel. In the three months we've been dating, The Scarlet Lady has become our spot. A big open room with TVs bolted above the double rack of bottles. There is no football game to watch tonight. The screens beam grainy crime scenes on mute. Tonight our favorite bartender is working, a masc with close cropped salt n' pepper hair and a thick dog chain around their neck. I sip my tequila and watch the neon sign above the door click on and off. Every time the door opens, I look for Heidi.

The room fills fast when the huge clock on the wall hits nine. Already there's a long queue for karaoke. The stage, a small blue square framed by beer pennants. In the chalky haze of the spotlight, Heidi sings about stars. I stand by the bar and snap pictures. The phone's flash reflects off her red "Ohio Against the World" shirt, and it makes her look as if she's blushing when she sings, *I can hardly wait to be with you again.* The Carpenters' tender lyrics do make me blush. But Heidi's voice is confident when the chorus comes, sure in its tenderness: *Don't you remember, you told me you loved me, baby?* The crowd sings along.

The song ends, and we hold hands under a crisp black flag that reads: *This is Saints Country.* I ask her, *Do you think everyone here is from the South or Midwest?* She sips her beer. *A girl can dream.* I smile, push my straw deep into the ice trying to find one last pocket of tonic. A man in a Saints jersey leans over his chair back to tell Heidi, *You have the voice of an angel.* She tucks her hands under her chin, bats her eyes: *This old thing?* Everyone laughs. She tells me, *The Carpenters were one of my favorite bands when I was a kid. Karen is why I learned to play drums.* I say I also loved their music but don't mention my inspiration wasn't Karen's virtuosic drumming but a Lifetime biopic. As a teen, I imagined Karen Carpenter's songs as mini-movies set in her childhood home, a sun-soaked suburb less than thirty miles away from this very bar. I tell Heidi the songs are inseparable from the Southern California landscape for me. A place where hot, restless women with names like Karen and Joan sip lemon tea and sped down the freeways, cigarettes wedged between their lips.

When I tell Jess I miss the roof rat, she sends me a link to a local rattery's website, where I look at photos of blue-ribbon rats. In one picture, a rat raises its chin in the air as if posing. This rat, like every other fancy rat at Pacific Gems, is bred for human interaction. It can be trained to use a litter box and come when its name is called. As I zoom in on a young Dumbo rat the size of a pear, I imagine walking it to the beach on a bejeweled leash. A feed of late-night selfies, little Marguerite or Anaïs doleful on my shoulder. I consider it a point of pride that I can imagine such scenes without wincing. I don't tell Jess I'm still afraid of real rats. I miss the roof rat no less.

Sometimes I catch myself listening for it. The disconnect

between the pleasure I experience when I think about rats and the physical revulsion I experience upon encountering one off the page feels like betrayal. A personal failure. My mind wants sole control of my sense of disgust. My fear. I'll train myself.

I set out again. I go harder.

I follow social media feeds of pet rats. Bougie little Dumbos dressed in hand-stitched muumuus. White lace on white fur. I replay YouTube clips of lab rats giggling and purring, helping each other find food. In a GIF, a toddler kisses a pet rat between the whiskers. My chest tightens in fear. Even as I know the kiss likely brought them both real pleasure.

Pleasure, too, can be scary. I'm reminded of this fact every time I walk on my block and pass the truck with the license plate that reads: *1 MORE X*. As with everything I like, I crave more.

You could find me in a freeze frame, ass up on a rug, red lips spread, and I would feel little fear or embarrassment. Nothing about me specifically is being revealed by that image. Not so when Heidi pushes her knee between my thighs, and my legs splay open, too wide too soon, my hips hitching towards her, cunt sucking at empty air, impatient for her hand. I tremble, joy shot through with fear. My cosmic want. It goes on and on.

To me, there's nothing greedy about rats' constant hunger. They sniff the street, the air, each other, over and over. They want to know the contents of their world down to every molecule. Even if all they discover is more hunger: each other's. They're able to discern seven distinct organic chemicals present in other rats in varying levels depending on the contents of their belly. When they smell need, rats will share their food with other rats. They do it all the time.

Not like the birds in the marina, fighting over garlic fries outside 24/7 Shrimp. When we wake, they're squawking on the docks. Slimy gray clouds seal the sky. I can hear the water sloshing against the boats. Sunglasses pushed up my nose. On the hotel balcony, I smoke a spliff until it's gone. I can't do it any other way. Below, kids with red domed cheeks leap into a pool shaped like a palm frond, then push themselves out of the water, four hands flat against the concrete lip. Again, again, the youngest shouts.

"The best thing about the past is that it's over," writes Joanne Kyger in a poem I read on my phone. The sun is an oily streak on the screen. "When you die you wake up." I wake up. Black coffee in a small white cup.

I'm alive for the first time in months.

Tonight the moon fills my room, and I see its ugly orange

light through my closed eyelids. I kick off the sheets and swallow a sleeping pill. I wait for my limbs to tingle. Many years ago, this pill was tested on rats. In the U.S. more than 111 million rats and mice are used annually in U.S. biomedical research, primarily to develop drugs and explore behavior in psychology experiments.

On my phone, I read rat studies while I wait for sleep. Most of the studies are boring, full of chemical names I can't pronounce. Then I find an article about a team of Dutch neuroscientists who discovered that rats are altruistic. They avoid harming other rats whenever possible. The researchers learn this while searching for new drug treatments to increase harm aversion in patients who show psychopathic behavior. Scientists gave rats a choice between two levers they could press to receive candies. After the rats developed a preference for one lever, the scientists rewired the system so that pressing the favored lever sent an electric shock to the floor of a neighboring rat, which squeaked in distress. The rats stopped using their favorite lever to avoid hurting the other rat, even if the rat was a stranger. As I read, I'm struck by the rats' empathy. But the pleasure of this knowledge soon gives way to horror: sensitive rats are still shocked over and over. Worse: some are forced to do the shocking.

On the weekend, Heidi flies me to San Francisco, and we

speed up and down the hills on her blue Vespa. She wears a helmet that resembles a disco ball, and it casts shards of glittery light as we pass glass-walled bars and hair salons. At the pupuseria, Heidi tells me that the tech company she works for has an office in LA. They offered to transfer her next spring. "Nothing would make me happier," I say. We wipe green sauce from our mouths and zoom off. At the bar, I hug her friends in the red light. There are naked barbies glued to a chandelier white with dust. Heidi chats with the bartender, a butch in a bright button down and boston scally cap. *She used to work at the Lex before it closed.* I had read about the legendary lesbian bar in Michelle Tea's memoir *Valencia*, but never stepped foot inside myself. Early in our relationship, Heidi's connection to the Lex had impressed me: one of Heidi's ex-girlfriends had also been a bartender there and served drinks the night it closed. But, tonight, I'm happy to be here, with her, under the dusty chandelier. At a wobbly table, we swap stories with her friends about bar brawls and bad roommates. *Mine lets their dog shit all over the house,* someone says. *Mine plays loud music,* I say. On the sidewalk, I snap a blurry picture of Heidi in front of the bar's sign, an old telephone. "Cute to meeeee," I say, leaning in for a kiss.

My building hires a new security guard. He comes one starless night and tells me I can't smoke cigarettes on the roof. *Oh, I don't smoke,* I say, unsure who I'm trying to convince. I follow him down the stairs. He points me out the glass front door. Standing on the sidewalk, the glare of the port lights no longer distracts. I notice that the neighbors with the three loud dogs are watching a TV propped on a plastic crate. I can't tell what they're watching, but I can count the skateboards on the porch.

When pedestrians see me slouched against the stucco, they lower their gaze, scatter into the street. So do the rats I spy each night. They dart across the same stretch of asphalt, never straying from their predetermined path along the ridge of the gutter. I envy them. The comfort their routine brings. I wonder if my roof rat now lives in the palm in my neighbor's yard, looking down on me even now. I've been assuming it was captured, poisoned. But what if the rat simply left? I imagine the scene: it slides down the telephone wire, fur a blur across the street, into the fronds. Who wouldn't want to sleep in a crown of branches? Under a yellow moon? I wonder why it never occurred to me that it *could* leave. I text a biologist friend: *Do rats dream about the future?*

6. THE RATS ARE COMING

Spring 2020

I finally meet the rats in Heidi's backyard. I notice them first when I'm flatlined in her bed, nursing a migraine in the blue twilight of the TV. The pain started on my drive from LA to San Francisco in the car she rented for me so we can quarantine together at her house. She brings me tea in bed. On the TV, a murder mystery. The plot: a woman's legs splayed in the street. There is one black shoe laced on her foot. I can't make out her face. I'm not sure I'm supposed to see anything more than the hairy neck of a cop filling the frame. I feel seasick watching death portrayed this way, a tidy plot-line I can ride until the credits roll, when every intensive care unit in the city is full of people. The camera cuts to a close-up of a newspaper clipping, followed by a thick skid mark on a side street. The plot peaks when the detective connects the clues in his head. For him, the clarity is pure pleasure. My vision blurs. The room pulses in unison with my left temple. Every sound amplified. The static between commercials. The scratching on the shingles. I don't ask her, *Did you hear that?* I seek no outside confirmation. When I hear them scratching, I know I'm home.

If I dream about rats, I do not dream about the coronavirus. The state closes restaurants and beaches soon after I arrive in San Francisco. We count the days until our relocation to LA. I open an email from the library that says *furloughed* six times. An ad for yoga pants tells me: "Find comfort in these trying times." Some friends think I'm in LA at the apartment with Mark. They send me articles with titles like "101 Ways to Survive Lockdown When Your Living Situation Is Unsafe."

I wake too early and open my phone. On my feed, a picture of Mark and Sean drinking home brew in the courtyard of our apartment. The caption reads, "Stay home! Protect yourself and others!" I shut off my phone. My intestines cramp all the same. If I were not in San Francisco, would I be there with them, smiling in the frame? I wonder if I would've posted the same photo on my feeds: "So much sun!" My stomach is too weak to eat the rest of the day.

If Heidi had not said, "Come stay with me." If she had not rented the car for me to drive 406 miles North on I-5 in the rain. If she had not kissed me when I walked through her front door and tossed my bags on her floor.

I never allowed myself to say, "I feel unsafe here with him." If I said it aloud, my fear would become a verifiable fact.

Every day I open a book, scroll the news, watch documentaries of black and white archival footage. I gather facts for fun. I move them around the page for big pleasure. But I don't know what to do with this particular personal fact.

The pea flowers on the vine outside the window tell me it's spring, but I don't believe them, or the sun shining longer and longer into the evening. What does the sun know?

The first few weeks in San Francisco I do little more than read in the weeds out back. I drink milky tea from a chipped cup. On the fence, pink trumpets shudder in the wind. I watch hummingbirds come and suck nectar, wings beating, beating. On my bench, I sit in ripped tights, lays splayed. I catch myself feeling *relaxed* for the first time in months.

Jess and Rachel send me other dispatches from the field. News articles with big black titles: "Angry and Cannibalistic, America's Rats Are Getting Desperate" and "Local Wildlife Thrives Amid Lockdown." They've watched me read about rats on the bus, at the beach, in the bar. They've witnessed me glory in the rat life: *When they're not eating, they're fucking!* On the first warm evening of the season, a friend texts me a grainy video of her backyard overgrown with avocado trees. I watch a blurry branch shake. A rat enters the frame. It jumps from one skinny branch onto an even skinnier power line, then disappears.

"Rats May Proliferate During the Pandemic." This narrative pleases me: slutty city rats go wild with no humans to break their revelry. But I've seen the old rats myself. Like so many tiny bodies of power: already-always there.

In bed Heidi sleeps late. I lace my high-tops and walk up a steep street, deserted at dawn save for the pigeons. With the freeways empty, the sky is clear. I don't recognize it most days, so accustomed to the smog. It's too blue. A trick, this clarity.

Late afternoon rain comes and knocks the little white flowers off the tea tree. A fresh dusting for the rats.

At night I dream I'm driving a red car with white leather seats splattered with blood. On the floorboard is a tangle of sheer pantyhose. There are thick black gloves on my hands. When I open the trunk, blood sloshes out the sides. I realize, in horror, that I'm not the victim in this narrative. In this one, I'm driving the plot.

Over eggs and toast, I tell Heidi, *The murder shows are fucking with my brain.* I stop watching the mysteries and switch to reality TV. I dive deep into the archives. On the

TLC docu-reality show *My Strange Addiction*, a woman named Carrie Steele proudly drinks her own urine, claiming the practice has cured her skin cancer. Of all the benefits of her magical self-cure, she repeats the word "free."

When I watch Carrie Steele brush her teeth with pee, my fur stands up. But in a nation where one-quarter of patients diagnosed with cancer can't afford treatment, I can't deny the appeal of her self-therapy.

I flip to a talk show. A self-professed healer who tells me I can protect myself against the coronavirus by taking high doses of melatonin. Studies are being conducted to test the hormone's potent anti-inflammatory effects, she assures me. I turn off the TV.

Books pile around the bed. I work my way through them like a rat rooting through a trash bag. Unlike the rat, I don't want to come out the other end. I have little use for the moonlight these days. Any stars. It's a shock to walk out into the night and discover this beauty isn't enough.

It's the end of the month, and I want to spend the last twenty dollars in my bank account on cigarettes and melons in a bright green sack. On the steps, we watch two men across the street push a busted recliner onto the sidewalk. Beside the recliner, there's a big green book with the words *Wheels Throughout History* written on the cover and a box of muscle car magazines tied with blue string. I imagine hopping in one of the little pink Corvettes in the magazines and driving back to LA, down to Laguna to tour the bars.

I kick my legs out in the crabgrass. A bird motionless on a fence, then in the air. Its confidence startles me. The lizard is sunning on a brick by our door. If it tries to catch any flies, I don't notice. I'm not against staying here. With her. Our lizard. I'm not against remaking the week, the world in my head. Clouds pass over us. We slice limes and wait for the cicadas. We can't hear them above the neighbor's TV. Our gossip about the neighbors.

April comes, and there are new neighbors to gossip about. We move to the Palms neighborhood in the heart of LA. We pick it off a map: so close to Heidi's new office. Also, rats. The eternal promise of palm trees.

In our yard, there are no palms. I tend the lantanas, deadheading through the afternoon. A pomelo tree blocks the bedroom window, obscuring the freeway. Some days I forget I live in the city. I sleep later and later into the mornings, and in the evenings, we peel pomelos on the stoop. The melons are small, still firm, but sweet enough to wait for.

Late May: my phone usage is up 87%. But I don't watch the video footage of George Floyd's murder by the Minneapolis police. There are limits to what watching can do for me. At the Black Lives Matter protest in Hollywood, I stand close to strangers' bodies for the first time in months.

Wildfire season. With her, I go back to the desert. We stay at her cabin in Morongo Valley. The hillside black beyond the greasewood. We don't hike. We wander through yuccas with beer in our bag. Big bossy clouds wall off the sky. In a red canyon, a woman with a dog wants us to stop, sniff the black bush. She shows us how to do it: lean close, blow on the bush, inhale hard. We do as she instructs. We smell smoke and smile. We ask her the name of the bush. She shrugs. The bark looks as if it's painted on with a brush.

On Box Canyon Road, we stop to photograph the purple mountains. Heidi stands in a wash, dwarfed by two massive transmission towers, camera slung around her neck. *Do you hear that?* she asks. *Listen.* I do. The towers are crackling.

There are no stars, not any night this week. Neither of us minds. In the cabin's solar box, I find other bright signs.

Someone has piled twigs and cholla spines in the box, obscuring the batteries. With old grill tongs, I remove the debris. I discover loose screws, cigarette butts, chunks of bark, paper, and bone. I pull out a gold gum foil. I'm dismantling the nest of a master archivist.

I type into my phone: *What animal makes a nest of junk?* I'm embarrassed I didn't guess the architects myself: desert rats. I spread their treasures on the dirt. In the haul, I spy my lost zippo lighter. It glistens in the moonlight. As I soon learn, desert woodrats protect themselves and their history by peeing on their nests. The sugar in their viscous urine crystalizes the nest as it dries, forming a stiffened nest called a midden, preserving the twigs, seeds, and everything else inside for thousands of years.

Nestled in the shelter of a rock, tree, or building, rat middens can be three to six feet high and eight feet across. If left undisturbed, generations of rats will eat, sleep, and piss in the same midden. Well-preserved middens contain fragments of ancient DNA. Because the foraging range of rats is limited, the contents of their nests give unparalleled insight into their local environments. Increasingly, scientists are turning to fossilized middens for clues about past climatic changes and how living organisms coped. In Colorado researchers are charting the changes in the timberline over the past 3,000 years using midden fragments. As recently as 2019, scientists discovered the oldest known papillomavirus in a 27,000-year-old midden in the Grand Canyon.

Middens may be invaluable portals to the past, but I refuse to be seduced by narratives that spotlight rat's usefulness. I resist the premise that rats have a right to exist only if they produce value to human society. I keep a love note tacked above my desk: *You are worth so much more than your productivity.*

Golden poppies push through my brain when I read about the woodrats' advanced archival techniques. Several of my friends have sustained themselves, their bodies and their apartments, with pee. Some posted ads for "goddess nectar" online, then froze their pee in airtight Tupperware, and mailed it to paying customers across the heartland. Others drove themselves downtown to a candlelit dungeon where they spread their legs and showered naked men and women with golden light and left with envelopes of cash. Others smeared it across their cheeks to slough away their dead winter faces. They dabbed it on their neck as a DIY anti-aging serum. Drank it to soothe their ulcer, or so they hoped.

Cold sweat in bed, head quaking, I'll pursue any route to relief. Stinky root teas. LSD. Bone broth. Lavender-stuffed pillowcases. Anti-seizure sprinkle capsules. If I believed my own urine could drown out my migraines, I would drink it by the pot.

The origins of urine therapy are largely attributed to Indian culture, though it's currently practiced across the world from China to America. The Damar Tantra, an ancient Sanskrit text, suggests that drinking one's own urine can prevent and even cure everything from indigestion to rosacea. Pliny the Elder and Madonna have recommended it as an antifungal.

In America, the primary popularizer of urine therapy was John W. Armstrong, whose influential treatise *The Water of Life* was published in 1944. According to Armstrong, anyone could achieve better health without doctors. All they had to do was spread their legs and let their powers flow.

In one passage, Armstrong advises a woman suffering from painful periods to drink her own urine "heavily overcharged with menstrual blood." Which sounds like performance art I might want to see.

The man at the hardware store doesn't mention crystalized middens when he lists the red flags of rat infestation. I ask him if there are any "good ways" to get rid of woodrats. His eyes lift: *You from around here?* Heidi says, *LA.* He guides us to an aisle with baits and traps. *The good news*, he says, *woodrats are easy to control.* Unlike city rats. Once a rat sees its nest mate crushed in a trap, it remembers.

ACTIVE INGREDIENT: Bromethalin (CAS #63333-35-7): . . 0.01%
OTHER INGREDIENTS…99.99%

One aisle over from the traps, we discover poison offers no kinder alternative. Bait manufacturers don't even list the specific ingredients on the back of the black box as if their death doesn't matter. The woodrat's death, like its life, is to remain a mystery.

I walk out the door with more questions than when I arrived.

Most days, I leave the desert's violence and beauty behind. Sitting on a warm, flat rock in the yard, I read news archives on my phone. I'm back at the beach, smoking on a barstool at the Little Shrimp, scheming to stop oil drilling off the Laguna coast, Bob Gentry at my side.

Heidi stacks the wood in the pit, strikes a match. *Look at the sunset*, she says. I glance up from the article: fat red line above the ridge. I look back down. *See the smoke rising.* The flames shoot, yellow flashes rise beyond my screen. *Uh huh*, I say, eyes fixed on the paragraph, searching for the end so I can begin again. The moon rising over the ridge. I look up. Where else am I trying to get?

On our last day, I leave a note pinned under a rock for the

rat. It has a habit of taking pages from unattended books. *Don't worry*, I tell Heidi, *I'm not trying to communicate with it.* I don't want the rat to read my words. I want it to take my words back to its nest, pee all over them, and remake them into a new world.

Back in Palms, the pomelo tree pushes against our bedroom window. Under the tree, melons juice themselves in the dirt. Three dark rings. I inspect the melons with new suspicion. Last night a neighbor taped a note to our front door that reads: *Please inform your landlord your property has rats. We've seen them coming our way on our security cameras.* There was no signature or return address. The author's terseness did not bother me. How had I failed to notice all those rats rushing the neighbor's gates? *Look again*, I tell myself.

Two days later, the neighbor's security camera records this scene: a woman in white high-tops walks onto the sidewalk. She is carrying a black bag of trash. Her face twists like a used paper towel. A dark blot with a tail streaks across the bottom of the screen. The woman throws the trash bag. She stands. She stands and shakes.

Once I thought my one true skill was the ability to reimagine my way out of any unsavory situation. But back then, I was easily confused.

A tragedy: I cannot read, or romanticize, my way out of every fear. What's worse: I'm no longer sure I want to.

After all this time, my story won't convince my body, shaking for everyone and the Ring camera to see.

At night my pinkie numbs holding my phone while I watch videos of rats dragging slices of pizza through New York City streets. Even after I put my phone down, my pinkie tingles and tingles. I search *nerve damage from holding phone*. My fingers throb as I read the words *permanent numbness*. I put the phone down, then pick it up. I read further. Fear helps protect us, I'm told. It makes us alert to danger and prepares us to deal with it. I repeat this to myself until I believe it.

In the morning, two men in white come and buzz down the trees in the yard, branch by branch. Later I listen through the walls to our next-door neighbors on the phone with the landlord. *We loved those trees*, they say. *We saw no rats.* I wonder how they didn't notice the fur or the tails. I try to decide whether this makes them lucky.

I, too, miss the trees.

On *The Real Housewives of Orange County*, every yard teems with fruit trees. The sun sets bright gold over the ocean. We watch the gold come and go every night. A stream of white-blonde hair and cleavage so deep I lose myself in its crevices. Whole weeks dissolve.

I no longer take comfort in discernment. As news stories pile in my feed, I cling to the housewives' every word. *Did Tamra give Vickie's new boyfriend the evil eye*, I ask Heidi. It's a relief to debate and critique things with no stake in the present.

At 2am the freeway is quiet. On the green couch, I listen to the wind lift the curtains. I scan the day's headlines on my phone, slowing when I see the lead in the *OC Register*: "Historic Main Street Bar & Cabaret's windows smashed by an apparent Molotov cocktail." My heart beats fast, as if I saw a rat. Is this attack a sign the gay scene in Laguna is dead, or alive?

With museums and bars closed, my plan to show Heidi the real Orange County devolves into a tour of parking lots. At a strip mall in Anaheim, we idle before a liquor store with a blinking palm on the sign, its drunken dance jerky and gleeful. *Here is where I like to read*, I tell her: the back edge of a Chase Bank in Garden Grove where a lesbian bar once stood. We kiss in its honor. We can't get inside the chained lot at Newport High, so I stick my hand through a metal slit and point to the strip of concrete where students gathered two years ago to protest the school's decades-long rat problem. The park off Logan Street where over 500 Latinx tenants organized rent strikes in 1985. The sidewalk outside the Cabaret where I promise to buy her a martini when the city opens. *I'll tip the bartender a fifty*, she says. I believe her. At the burger stall, we order milkshakes and fries. We eat as we drive. I trace our names in the Styrofoam cup with my fingernail. A big dumb smiley face. Parked on a side street outside the Boom Boom Room, where Paul Lynde once laughed and kissed and vomited vodka, she pins me to the passenger seat. I peel my thong off in the shadow of a cell phone tower disguised as a palm tree, or is it a real palm tree? I can't tell, but the branches shake the same in the breeze. The wind blows the joint out when I pass it to her. I pull her braids loose with one rough finger.

Back home, the pomelos are gone and the trees are cut, but the rats still scratch in the bedroom wall. In the kitchen, she places plates on the table and calls my name, but I linger, lean against the window waiting to see the rat's face when it shoots out the hole and finds its beloved tree gone, nowhere left to hide, the shock of unfettered moonlight. Does it tremble? Does it walk boldly off into the night? Knowing what I know about my friends, I suspect they will prevail. But I don't hang around to find out. She calls my name. I sit down at the table and eat.

SELECTED BIBLIOGRAPHY

BOOKS

Aldous Huxley, *Tomorrow, Tomorrow, Tomorrow*

Alejandra Pizarnik, *Extracting the Stone of Madness: Poems 1962 – 1972*, trans. Yvette Siegert

Amina Cain, *Indelicacy*

Brenda Hillman, *Bright Existence*

Dolores Hayden, *The Grand Domestic Revolution: A History of Feminist Designs for American Homes, Neighborhoods, and Cities*

E.B. White, *Charlotte's Web*

Gustavo Arellano, *Orange County: A memoir*

Hal Fischer, *The Gay Seventies*

John W. Armstrong, *The Water of Life*

Lisa McGirr, *Suburban Warriors: The Origins of the New American Right*

Nicholas Schou, *Orange Sunshine: The Brotherhood of Eternal Love and Its Quest to Spread Peace, Love, and Acid to *the World*

Robert Hendrickson, *More Cunning than Man: A Social History of Rats and Men*

Robert Sullivan, *Rats: Observations on the History & Habitat of the City's Most Unwanted Inhabitants*

<u>ARTICLES</u>

Andrea Richards. "Rats? In my house? Say it ain't so." *Los Angeles Magazine*. February 14, 2017.

Associated Press. "San Francisco says homeless encampment a health hazard, wants it shut down." *Los Angeles Times*. February 26, 2016.

Benjamin Oreskes. "Desperate to get rid of homeless people, some are using prickly plants, fences, barriers." *Los Angeles Times*. July 10, 2019.

Benjamin Oreskes and David Zahniser. "L.A. is uneasy about order to move homeless people from freeways. 'There's ethical issues.'" *Los Angeles Times*. May 20, 2020.

Benjamin Oreskes and Doug Smith. "Homelessness jumps 12% in L.A. County and 16% in the city; officials 'stunned." *Los Angeles Times*. June 4, 2019.

Bryce Alderton. "Judge won't block Laguna's homeless laws while ACLU lawsuit is pending." *Los Angeles Times*. February 18, 2016.

Dakota Smith. "Garcetti faces heat over L.A.'s homeless crisis but remains optimistic. Is he being realistic?" *Los Angeles Times*. June 6, 2019.

Dakota Smith and David Zahniser. "Filth from homeless camps is luring rats to L.A. City Hall, report says." *Los Angeles Times*. June 3, 2019.

Dartunorro Clark. "Angry and Cannibalistic, America's Rats Are Getting Desperate.' NBC News. April 13, 2020.

David Zahniser. "L.A. exposed city workers to trash, bodily fluids outside City Hall East, state says." *Los Angeles Times*. August 15, 2019.

Dianne Klein. "For Laguna Beach's Mayor, a Private Grief Goes Public: Bob Gentry: 'Losing Gary (Burdick, above) is very devastating." *Los Angeles Times*. February 1, 1989.

Donna Littlejohn. "Deputy LA City Attorney in San Pedro goes public with typhus bout, prompting City Hall to take notice." *The Daily Breeze*. February 7, 2019.

Doug Smith. "Does L.A. count its homeless, or make its best guess? A little of both, it turns out." *Los Angeles Times*. August 18, 2020.

Emily Alpert Reyes. "L.A. city, county OK homeless plans, but where will the money come from?" Abby Sewell, *Los Angeles Times*. February. 9, 2016.

Emily Alpert Reyes. "Protesters surround tents, block

streets to stop major cleanup of Hollywood homeless encampment." *Los Angeles Times*. August 26, 2020.

Emily Alpert Reyes. "With L.A. City Hall infested by rats, one councilman cites homeless crisis." *Los Angeles Times*. February 8, 2019.

Erika I. Ritchie. "Historic Coast Inn remodel approved by Laguna Beach council after developer makes concessions." T*he Orange County Register*. July 29, 2020.

Erika I. Ritchie. "Historic Main Street Bar & Cabaret's windows smashed by an apparent Molotov cocktail." *The Orange County Register*. July 24, 2020.

Faith E. Pinho. "Laguna's former Boom Boom Room slated to become Bear Flag Fish Co." *Los Angeles Times*. August 14, 2019.

Gale Holland and Dakota Smith. "L.A. agreed to let homeless people keep their skid row belongings. That could change." *Los Angeles Time*s. July 5, 2019.

Gale Holland and David Zahniser. "L.A. agrees to let homeless people keep skid row property — and some in downtown aren't happy," *Los Angeles Times*. May 29, 2019.

Gale Holland. "Racism is the reason Black people are disproportionately homeless in L.A. report shows." *Los Angeles Times*. June 12, 2020.

Joanna Clay. "Where has Laguna's gay dynamic gone?" *The*

Orange County Register. August 8, 2013.

Jodie Tillman and Leonard Ortiz. "Gay Old Time: The rise and fall of Laguna Beach's gay clubs." *The Orange County Register*. January 11, 2018.

Jodie Tillman. "Breathing life back into Laguna Beach's gay bar scene." *The Orange County Register*. May 14, 2016.

Leslie Earnest. "No More Cheers as Little Shrimp Faces Last Call: Landmark: Monday's closing of Laguna Beach's longtime gay hangout saddens its customers." *Los Angeles Times*. May 28, 1995.

Louis Sahagun. "Coyotes, falcons, deer, and other wildlife are reclaiming L.A. territory as humans stay at home." *Los Angeles Times*. April 21, 2020.

Marion Renault. "Reading the Past in Old, Urine-Caked Rat's Nests," *New York Times*. February 20, 2020.

Meghan Lamb. "I cut and cut and cut away: an interview with Kate Zambreno." *Los Angeles Review of Books*. February 13, 2017.

Myriam Gurba. "From Persephone to Tara Reade, rape victims are relegated to everyday hells." *Luz Collective*. December 9, 2020.

Nancy Luna. "Woody's in Laguna to close." *The Orange County Register*. January 4, 2007.

Nate Jackson. "Laguna's Legendary Boom Boom Room Returns for One Night Only on New Year's Eve." *OC*

Weekly. December 30, 2017.

Nita Lelyveld. "City Beat: The homeless make us ashamed and angry — at our city and at ourselves." *Los Angeles Times*. June 6, 2019.

OC Weekly Staff. "The State of LGBT OC by a City Councilman and the Former Mayor of West Hollywood." *OC Weekly*. August 8, 2013.

Orange County Register Staff. "One last toast at the Boom Boom Room." *The Orange County Register*. September 3, 2007.

Stacy Hardy. "An Aesthetics Of Rat Bites." *Joyland*. April 12, 2017.

Steve Lopez. "Column: There's a trash and rodent nightmare in downtown L.A., with plenty of blame to go around." *Los Angeles Times*. May 25, 2019.

Tammerlin Drummond. "For Robert Gentry, This Was a Year of Picking Up the Pieces : Profile: The Laguna Beach mayor saw his longtime companion die of AIDS, and he was continually asked about his own health." *Los Angeles Times*. December 5, 1989.

ACKNOWLEDGEMENTS

Thank you to the rats in the roof, the wall, the solar box. Without you, nothing.

To Kristin Sanders, Allie Rowbottom, Amanda Montei, Caroline Crew, Lindsey Webb, Corinna Cook, Chris Daley, and Daphne Sidor for giving encouragement and insightful feedback on early drafts.

To all the friends who sent me rat stories, pics, dreams, nightmares, and news articles. I saved every shot of every hollowed orange.

To Rebecca and Sol for late nite karaoke, loose ham, and many hot tub convos about rats and everything else under the desert stars.

Thank you to *Cream City Review*, *Peach Mag*, *Pleiades*, *Salty Mag*, and *The Iowa Review* for providing a supportive home for excerpts from this book.

To Heidi who will never ask me to trade my violets for roses. For moonrises on the hill, Sand to Snow nights, fireside jokes, Guns n Roses, and big romance.

ABOUT THE AUTHOR

Elizabeth Hall is the author of *I Have Devoted My Life to the Clitoris*, a Lambda Literary Award Finalist. Her nonfiction work has appeared in *Bon Appétit*, *Black Warrior Review*, *Electric Literature*, the *Iowa Review*, *Pleiades Magazine*, and elsewhere.